About the author:

From Perth, Western Australia, Lisa Van Der Wielen graduated
from University with a Bachelor of education. Being a dedicated
primary school teacher and having a passion for writing, lead her to
become a children's author, with her first book
Vegetarian Polony being published in 2017.

Her love for the beach, nature, dogs, family and the
importance of virtues, provide her with inspiration to write
fun, rhyming tales that encourage children to learn, laugh
and enjoy the magic of reading.

A CIP catalogue record for this title is available from the British Library.

ISBN 978-1-5272-2863-4
(paper back)

First Published (2018)

To Mum and Dad

Luna Lucy

Author
Lisa Van Der Wielen

Illustrator
Joseph Hopkins

There once was a girl called Lucy,
who was crazy about the moon.
Every night she would sit by her front porch,
with her beloved dog Neptune.

Together they would sit and cuddle, wrapped up like a cocoon.
Gazing into the night sky, searching for the moon.

One day Lucy and Neptune were nestled on the front porch,
when Lucy couldn't see the moon even with her torch.

"Where is the moon?" she gasped. "It seems to have disappeared!"
She went to tell her Dad, to which he volunteered.

"The moon has many phases Lucy, just you wait and see.
Every night we will draw the moon and watch it change gradually."

So every night Lucy and her Dad drew a picture of the moon.
She waited for the darkness to fall every afternoon.

First the moon looked like the letter 'C',
Thin and half round like the shape of a pea.

Then after a few days the moon began to change.
The 'C' grew to a crescent shape.
How very strange.

Then as the week passed, the moon grew to a half.
It looked like a pizza, or part of a graph.

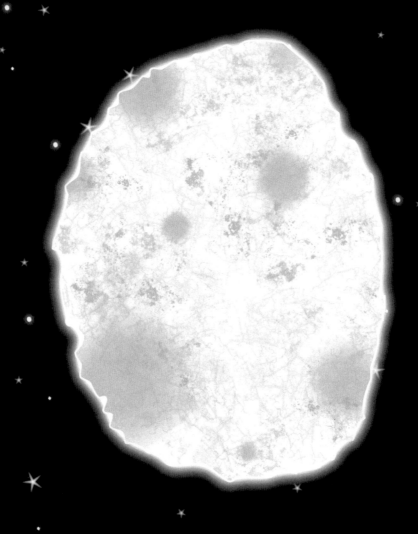

The next week the moon grew bigger,
it was almost looking round.
But some of the moon was still missing,
nowhere to be found.

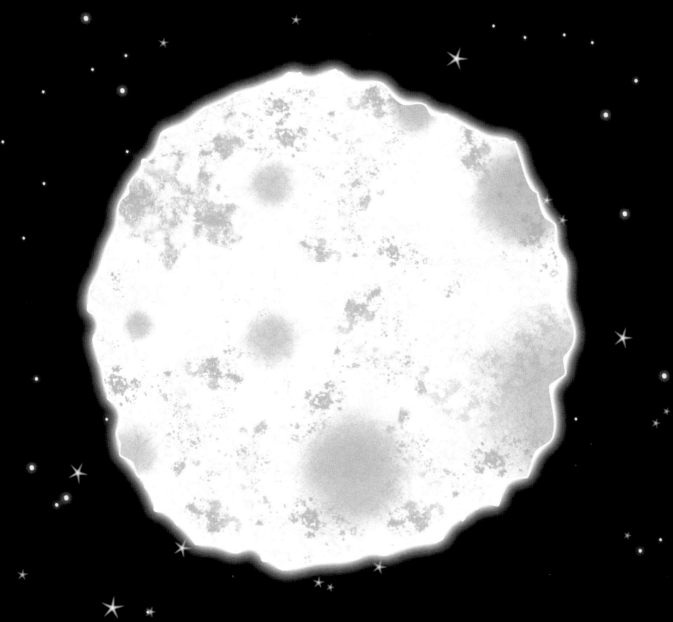

Then finally it happened, in the darkness way up high.
The moon was big and round,
brightening up the sky.

Pearly and circled was the big white moon,
lighting up the sky in the shape of a balloon.

Lucy cuddled Neptune while drawing in her sketchbook,
with a smile on her face and a delighted look.

Finally the moon was there for all to see,
in its perfectly round, pearly, white glory.

But it was only a few days when the moon began to change.
Its shape was slightly smaller, almost oval at long range.

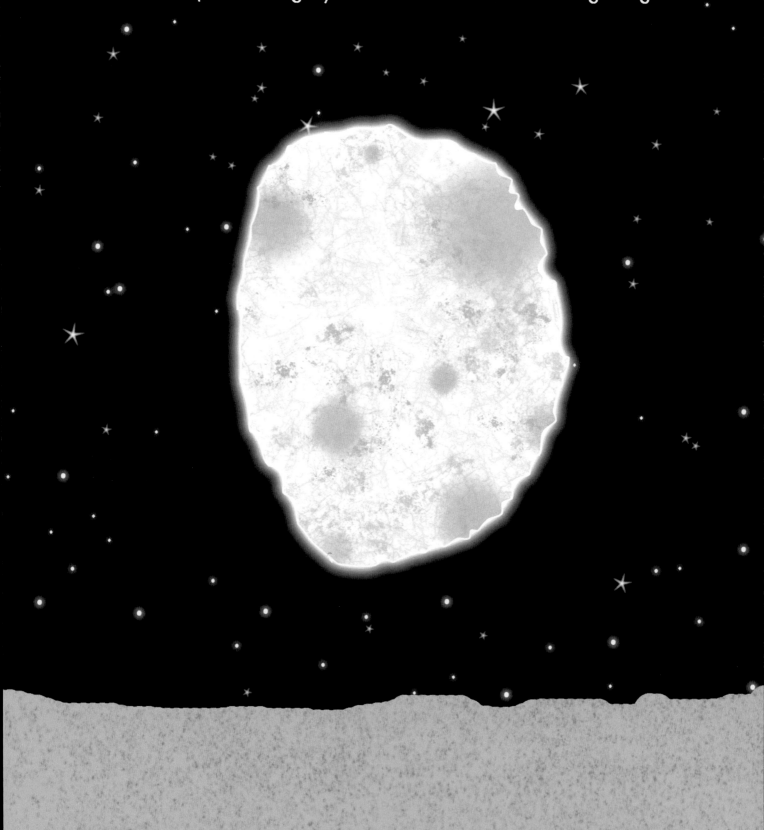

In just days it was smaller, now looking like a half,
except this time the pizza shape, was the other side of the graph.

By the end of that week the moon was higher than the tree.
It had turned into a letter shape,
Except a backward 'C'.

Then in just a few days,
the moon had disappeared.
The sky was dark and empty,
looking very weird.

"Don't worry," said Lucy's Dad.
"It's just the new moon phase,
the moon will start the cycle,
again in a few days."

Lucy looked back through her book,
of moon drawings she did everyday.
All because she thought,
the moon had gone away.

Lucy was now proud that she had created her own book.
She was excited to give everyone a look.

W X Y Z

So off she went to school
to share the book some more.
Everyone was listening,
sitting on the floor.

Everybody learnt about the phases of the moon,
when Lucy read her book called 'Luna Lucy and Neptune'.

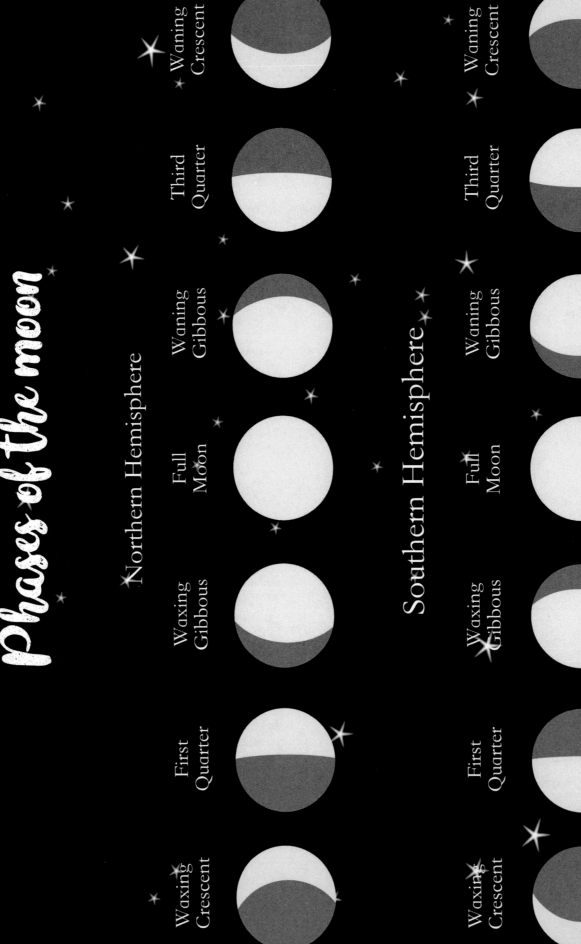

Check out Lisa Van der Wielen's amazing book

Instagram: @lisa.vanderwielen

Made in the USA
Coppell, TX
25 November 2020